Alfred Tennyson, Imogen Clark

Tennyson Year Book

Selections for Every day in the year from the poetry of Alfred Tennyson

Alfred Tennyson, Imogen Clark

Tennyson Year Book
Selections for Every day in the year from the poetry of Alfred Tennyson

ISBN/EAN: 9783337275358

Printed in Europe, USA, Canada, Australia, Japan

Cover: Foto ©Andreas Hilbeck / pixelio.de

More available books at **www.hansebooks.com**

TENNYSON YEAR BOOK

SELECTIONS
FOR EVERY DAY IN THE YEAR
FROM THE POETRY OF
ALFRED TENNYSON

BY

IMOGEN CLARK

*I held it truth, with him who sings
To one clear harp in divers tones,
That men may rise on stepping-stones
Of their dead selves to higher things.*
IN MEMORIAM, I

NEW-YORK
E. P. DUTTON & COMPANY
31 WEST TWENTY-THIRD STREET
1894

JANUARY.

Hope smiles from the threshold of the year to come,
Whispering, "It will be happier."

THE FORESTERS.

TENNYSON YEAR BOOK.

January First.

Well I know
That unto him who works, and feels he works,
This same grand year is ever at the doors.

The Golden Year.

January Second.

Ring in the valiant man and free,
The larger heart, the kindlier hand ;
Ring out the darkness of the land,
Ring in the Christ that is to be.

In Memoriam, cvi.

3

January Third.

We will walk this world
Yoked in all exercise of noble end;
And so thro' those dark gates across the wild
That no man knows.

The Princess.

January Fourth.

Fiercely flies
The blast of North and East, and ice
Makes daggers at the sharpen'd eaves.

In Memoriam, cvii.

January Fifth.

Human forgiveness touches Heaven and
thence
Reflected, sends a light on the forgiven.

Romney's Remorse.

January Sixth.

What use to brood ?   This life of mingled
    pains
        And joys to me,
Despite of every Faith and Creed, remains
        The Mystery.

                    To Mary Boyle.

January Seventh.

Behold, we know not anything ;
    I can but trust that good shall fall
    At last—far off—at last to all,
And every winter change to spring.

              In Memoriam, liv.

January Eighth.

I have not made the world, and He that
    made it will guide.

                      Maud.

January Ninth.

Yet Hope shall be the star that lights our
    night of grief on earth;
And she shall point to sweeter morns, when
    brighter suns shall rise,
And spread the radiance of their rays o'er
    earth, and seas, and skies.

> *"How gayly sinks the gorgeous sun*
> *within his golden bed."*

January Tenth.

No help but prayer,
A breath that fleets beyond this iron world,
And touches Him that made it.

Harold.

January Eleventh.

The face of Death is toward the Sun of Life,
His shadow darkens earth: his truer name

Is " Onward," no discordance in the roll
And march of that Eternal Harmony
Whereto the worlds beat time, though faintly
 heard,
Until the great Hereafter. Mourn in hope!

*The Death of the Duke of Clarence
and Avondale.*

January Twelfth.

If you fear
Cast all your cares on God; that anchor
 holds.

Enoch Arden.

January Thirteenth.

And murmurs of a deeper voice,
 Going before to some far shrine,
Teach that sick heart the stronger choice,
 Till all thy life one way incline
 With one wide will that closes thine.

On a Mourner.

January Fourteenth.

God gives us love.   Something to love
   He lends us; but when love is grown
To ripeness, that on which it throve
   Falls off, and love is left alone.

To J. S.

January Fifteenth.

I hold it true, whate'er befall;
   I feel it, when I sorrow most;
   'Tis better to have loved and lost
Than never to have loved at all.

In Memoriam, xxvii.

January Sixteenth.

The soul, th' eternal soul, must reign
   In worlds devoid of pain and strife;
Then why should mortal man complain
   Of death, which leads to happier life?

"Why should we weep for those who die?"

January Seventeenth.

Thou wilt not leave us in the dust:
Thou madest man, he knows not why;
He thinks he was not made to die;
And Thou hast made him: Thou art just.

In Memoriam.

January Eighteenth.

Fear not thou the hidden purpose of that
Power which alone is great,
Nor the myriad world, His shadow, nor the
silent Opener of the gate.

God and the Universe.

January Nineteenth.

He that ever following her commands,
On with toil of heart and knees and hands,

Through the long gorge to the far light, has
   won
His path upward, and prevailed,
Shall find the toppling crags of Duty scaled
Are close upon the shining table-lands
To which our God Himself is moon and sun.
          Ode on the Death of the Duke of Wellington.

January Twentieth.

Shall sharpest pathos blight us, knowing all
Life needs for life is possible to will.
          Love and Duty.

January Twenty-first.

Be thy heart a fortress to maintain
The day against the moment, and the year
Against the day.
          To the Duke of Argyll.

January Twenty-second.

Her faith is fixt and cannot move,
    She darkly feels him great and wise,
    She dwells on him with faithful eyes,
" I can not understand: I love."

                In Memoriam, xcvii.

January Twenty-third.

The more the love, the mightier is the prayer.
                Harold.

January Twenty-fourth.

Thou, from the first, unborn, undying love,
Albeit we gaze not on thy glories near,
Before the face of God didst breathe and
    move,
Tho' night and pain, and ruin and death reign
    here,
Thou foldest, like a golden atmosphere,
The very throne of the eternal God.

                Love.

January Twenty-fifth.

Forgive what seem'd my sin in me ;
    What seem'd my worth since I began ;
    For merit lives from man to man,
And not from man, O Lord, to Thee.

In Memoriam.

January Twenty-sixth.

Hurt no man more
Than you would harm your loving natural
    brother
Of the same roof, same breast.   If any do,
Albeit he think himself at home with God,
Of this be sure, he is whole worlds away.

Queen Mary.

January Twenty-seventh.

Uphold me, Father, in my loneliness
A little longer! Aid me, give me strength.

Enoch Arden.

January Twenty-eighth.

Thou canst not prove the Nameless, O my
    son,
Nor canst thou prove the world thou movest
    in.

The Ancient Sage.

January Twenty-ninth.

A height beyond the height!
Our hearing is not hearing,
And our seeing is not sight.

The Voice and the Peak.

January Thirtieth.

The sun, the moon, the stars, the seas, the
    hills and the plains—
Are not these, O Soul, the Vision of Him
    who reigns?

And the ear of man cannot hear, and the
    eye of man cannot see:
But if we could see and hear, this Vision—
    were it not He?

               The Higher Pantheism.

January Thirty-first.

How pure at heart and sound in head,
    With what divine affections bold,
    Should be the man whose thought would
        hold
An hour's communion with the dead.

In vain shalt thou, or any, call
    The spirits from their golden day,
    Except, like them, thou too canst say,
My spirit is at peace with all.

               In Memoriam, xciv.

FEBRUARY.

The silver tongue
Cold February loved.

THE BLACKBIRD.

February First.

Good will to me as well as all—
 I one of them: my brothers they:
Brothers in Christ—a world of peace
 And confidence day after day,
And trust and hope.

Supposed Confessions.

February Second.

I muse on joy that will not cease,
 Pure spaces clothed in living beams,
Pure lilies of eternal peace,
 Whose odors haunt my dreams.

Sir Galahad.

February Third.

But thou, O Lord,
Aid all this foolish people: let them take
Example, pattern: lead them to Thy light!

St. Simeon Stylites.

February Fourth.

Oh yet we trust that somehow good
    Will be the final goal of ill.

That nothing walks with aimless feet;
    That not one life shall be destroy'd,
    Or cast as rubbish to the void,
When God hath made the pile complete.

In Memoriam, liv.

February Fifth.

Sworn to vows
Of utter hardihood, utter gentleness,
And, loving, utter faithfulness in love,
And uttermost obedience to the King.

Gareth and Lynette.

February Sixth.

Often a man's own angry pride
    Is cap and bells for a fool.

Maud.

February Seventh.

If e'er when faith had fall'n asleep,
  I heard a voice, " Believe no more,"
  And heard an ever-breaking shore
That tumbled on the Godless deep;

A warmth within the breast would melt
  The freezing reason's colder part,
  And like a man in wrath the heart
Stood up and answer'd, " I have felt."

           In Memoriam, cxxiv.

February Eighth.

Knowledge is the swallow on the lake
That sees and stirs the surface-shadow there,
But never yet hath dipt into the abysm, . . .
For nothing worthy proving can be proven,
Nor yet disproven.

           The Ancient Sage.

February Ninth.

Faith has centre everywhere,
Nor cares to fix itself to form.

In Memoriam, xxxiii.

February Tenth.

A soul with no religion—
My mother used to say that such a one
Was without rudder, anchor, compass—
      might be
Blown every way with every gust, and wreck
On any rock.

The Promise of May.

February Eleventh.

A man is not as God,
But then most Godlike being most a man.

Love and Duty.

February Twelfth.

O Love, thy province were not large,
A bounded field, nor stretching far;
Look also, Love, a brooding star,
A rosy warmth from marge to marge.

In Memoriam, xlvi.

February Thirteenth.

Forward, forward let us range.
Let the great world spin forever down the
ringing grooves of change.

Locksley Hall.

February Fourteenth.

Love flew in at the window
As Wealth walk'd in at the door.
"You have come for you saw Wealth com-
ing," said I.

But he flutter'd his wings with a sweet little
cry,
" I'll cleave to you rich or poor."

The Foresters.

February Fifteenth.

We needs must love the highest when we
see it.

Guinevere.

February Sixteenth.

The churl in spirit, howe'er he veil
His want in forms for fashion's sake,
Will let his coltish nature break
At seasons thro' the gilded pale.

In Memoriam, cxi.

February Seventeenth.

Check every outflash, every ruder sally
Of thought and speech ; speak low.

Sonnet: "Check every outflash."

February Eighteenth.

So rich a fellowship
Would make me wholly blest: thou one of
them,
Be one indeed; consider them, and all
Their bearing in their common bond of love,
No more of hatred than in Heaven itself,
No more of jealousy than in Paradise.

Balin and Balan.

February Nineteenth.

I would the great world grew like thee,
Who grewest not alone in power
And knowledge, but by year and hour
In reverence and charity.

In Memoriam, cxiv.

February Twentieth.

Who loves not Knowledge? Who shall rail
Against her beauty? . . .
. . . Let her know her place;
She is the second, not the first.

In Memoriam, cxiv.

February Twenty-first.

Deep harm to disobey,
Seeing obedience is the bond of rule.

The Passing of Arthur.

February Twenty-second.

While the races of mankind endure,
Let his great example stand
Colossal, seen of every land,
And keep the soldier firm, the statesman
    pure;

Till in all lands and thro' all human story
The path of duty be the way to glory.

> *Ode on the Death of the Duke of Wellington.*

February Twenty-third.

Great in faith and strong
Against the grief of circumstance.

> *Supposed Confessions.*

February Twenty-fourth.

A lie which is all a lie may be met and fought
  with outright,
But a lie which is part a truth is a harder
  matter to fight.

> *The Grandmother.*

February Twenty-fifth.

Shall fears and jealous hatreds flame again?
  Or at thy coming, . . . everywhere,
  The blue heaven break, and some diviner
  air
Breathe thro' the world and change the hearts
  of men?

Duke and Duchess of Edinburgh.

February Twenty-sixth.

Not learned, save in gracious household
  ways,
Not perfect, nay, but full of tender wants,
No angel, but a dearer being, all dipt
In angel instincts, breathing Paradise.

The Princess.

February Twenty-seventh.

But thou be wise . . .
Nor take thy dial for thy deity,
But make the passing shadow serve thy will.

The Ancient Sage.

February Twenty-eighth.

Turn, Fortune, turn thy wheel and lower the
proud ;
Turn thy wild wheel thro' sunshine, storm
and cloud ;
Thy wheel and thee we neither love nor hate.

Smile and we smile, the lords of many lands ;
Frown and we smile, the lords of our own
hands ;
For man is man and master of his fate.

Enid.

February Twenty-ninth.

It is the low man thinks the woman low.
Sin is too dull to see beyond himself.

Queen Mary.

MARCH.

The windy gleams of March.

VIVIEN.

March First.

Dip down upon the northern shore,
　O sweet new-year delaying long;
　Thou doest expectant nature wrong;
Delaying long, delay no more.

In Memoriam, lxxxiii.

March Second.

For now the Heavenly Power
　Makes all things new,
And thaws the cold, and fills
　The flower with dew.

Early Spring.

March Third.

If Time be heavy on your hands,
Are there no beggars at your gate,
　Nor any poor about your lands?

Lady Clara Vere de Vere.

March Fourth.

Now fades the last long streak of snow,
    Now bourgeons every maze of quick
    About the flowering squares, and thick
By ashen roots the violets blow.

In Memoriam, cxv.

March Fifth.

He that only rules by terror
    Doeth grievous wrong.

The Captain.

March Sixth.

Are there thunders moaning in the distance?
Are there spectres moving in the darkness?
Trust the Hand of Light will lead her people,
Till the thunders pass, the spectres vanish,
And the Light is Victor.

Jubilee of Victoria.

March Seventh.

Let knowledge grow from more to more,
But more of reverence in us dwell;
That mind and soul, according well,
May make one music as before.

In Memoriam.

March Eighth.

One equal temper of heroic hearts,
Made weak by time and fate, but strong in
will
To strive, to seek, to find, and not to yield.

Ulysses.

March Ninth.

When rosy plumelets tuft the larch,
And rarely pipes the mounted thrush;
Or underneath the barren bush
Flits by the sea-blue bird of March.

In Memoriam, xci.

March Tenth.

Make Thou my spirit pure and clear
        As are the frosty skies,
Or this first snowdrop of the year
        That in my bosom lies.

St. Agnes.

March Eleventh.

It becomes no man to nurse despair,
But in the teeth of clench'd antagonisms
To follow up the worthiest till he die.

The Princess.

March Twelfth.

'Tis life, whereof our nerves are scant,
O life, not death, for which we pant;
More life, and fuller, that I want.

The Two Voices.

March Thirteenth.

Why should we weep for those who die?
  They fall—their dust returns to dust,
Their souls shall live eternally
  Within the mansions of the just.

  " Why should we weep for those who die ? "

March Fourteenth.

Peace; come away: the song of woe
  Is after all an earthly song.

  In Memoriam, lvii.

March Fifteenth.

Why not believe then?   Why not yet
Anchor thy frailty there, where man
Hath moored and rested?

  Supposed Confessions.

March Sixteenth.

The ground flame of the crocus breaks the
　　mould,
　Fair Spring slides hither o'er the Southern
　　sea,
Wavers on her thin stem the snowdrop cold
　That trembles not to kisses of the bee.

Progress of Spring.

March Seventeenth.

Whether
A mind be warm or cold, it serves to fan
A kindled fire.

Queen Mary.

March Eighteenth.

Anyhow, we must
Move in the line of least resistance when
The stronger motive rules.

The Promise of May.

March Nineteenth.

I stretch lame hands of faith, and grope,
And gather dust and chaff, and call
To what I feel is Lord of all,
And faintly trust the larger hope.

In Memoriam, lv.

March Twentieth.

Be wise,
Cleave ever to the sunnier side of doubt,
And cling to Faith beyond the forms of
Faith!
She reels not in the storm of warring words,
She brightens at the clash of "Yes" and
"No,"
She sees the Best that glimmers thro' the
Worst,
She feels the sun is hid but for a night,
She spies the summer thro' the winter bud.

The Ancient Sage.

March Twenty-first.

Give to the poor,
Ye give to God.   He is with us in the poor.

Queen Mary.

March Twenty-second.

The snowdrop only, flowering thro' the year,
Would make the world as blank as Winter-
tide.

The Last Tournament.

March Twenty-third.

O follow, leaping blood,
    The season's lure!
O heart, look down and up,
    Serene, secure,
Warm as the crocus cup,
    Like snowdrop pure!

Early Spring.

March Twenty-fourth.

And men have hopes which race the restless
    blood,
That after many changes may succeed
Life, which is Life indeed!

Progress of Spring.

March Twenty-fifth.

But the tongue is a fire, as you know, my
    dear, the tongue is a fire.

The Grandmother.

March Twenty-sixth.

His high sweet smile
In passing, and a transitory word
Make knight or churl, or child or damsel
    seem,
From being smiled at, happier in themselves.

Balin and Balan.

March Twenty-seventh.

Courtesy wins woman all as well
As valor may, but he that closes both
Is perfect.

The Last Tournament.

March Twenty-eighth.

Shall he for whose applause I strove,
  I had such reverence for his blame,
  See with clear eye some hidden shame,
And I be lessen'd in his love?

In Memoriam, li.

March Twenty-ninth.

There must be wisdom with great Death,
The dead shall look me thro' and thro'.

Be near us when we climb or fall;
  Ye watch, like God, the rolling hours
  With larger, other eyes than ours,
To make allowance for us all.

In Memoriam, li.

March Thirtieth.

Who knows the ways of the world, how God
    will bring them about ?

Maud.

March Thirty-first.

The Word had breath, and wrought
With human hands the creed of creeds
In loveliness of perfect deeds.

In Memoriam, xxxvi.

APRIL.

Sweet April wakes.

IN MEMORIAM, CXVI.

April First.

Come, Spring, for now from all the dripping
  eaves
The spear of ice has wept itself away,
And hour by hour unfolding woodbine leaves
  O'er his uncertain shadow droops the day.
                              Progress of Spring.

April Second.

The fire of Heaven has kill'd the barren cold,
And kindled all the plain and all the wold;
The new leaf ever pushes off the old.
                              Balin and Balan.

April Third.

I know that this was Life—the track
  Whereon with equal feet we fared;
  And then, as now, the day prepared
The daily burden for the back.
                              In Memoriam, xxv.

April Fourth.

Like souls that balance joy and pain,
With tears and smiles from heaven again
The maiden Spring upon the plain
Came in a sunlit fall of rain.
In crystal vapor everywhere,
Blue isles of heaven laugh'd between,
And far, in forest-deeps unseen,
The topmost elm tree gather'd green
From draughts of balmy air.

Sir Launcelot and Queen Guinevere.

April Fifth.

Howe'er it be, it seems to me,
'Tis only noble to be good.
Kind hearts are more than coronets,
And simple faith than Norman blood.

Lady Clara Vere de Vere.

April Sixth.

The old order changeth, yielding place to
new,
And God fulfils Himself in many ways,
Lest one good custom should corrupt the
world.

The Passing of Arthur.

April Seventh.

. . . The songs, the stirring air,
The life re-orient out of dust,
Cry thro' the sense to hearten trust
In that which made the world so fair.

In Memoriam, cxvi.

April Eighth.

The gay lent-lilies wave and put them by,
And out once more in varnish'd glory shine
Thy stars of celandine.

Progress of Spring.

April Ninth.

I found Him in the shining of the stars,
I mark'd Him in the flowering of His fields.

The Passing of Arthur.

April Tenth.

I too would teach the man
   Beyond the darker hour to see the bright,
That his fresh life may close as it began,
   The still-fulfilling promise of a light
   Narrowing the bounds of night.

Progress of Spring.

April Eleventh.

Our voices took a higher range;
   Once more we sang: "They do not die
   Nor lose their mortal sympathy,
Nor change to us, altho' they change."

In Memoriam, xxx.

April Twelfth.

Better not be at all
Than not be noble.

The Princess.

April Thirteenth.

Oh! what is so sweet as a morning in spring,
When the gale is all freshness, and larks, on
  the wing,
In clear, liquid carols their gratitude sing?

Huntsman's Song.

April Fourteenth.

Once more the Heavenly Power
  Makes all things new,
And domes the red-plow'd hills
  With loving blue;
The blackbirds have their wills,
  The throstles too.

Early Spring.

April Fifteenth.

Then let us join our feeble praise
To that which angels give ;
And hymns to that great Parent raise
In whom we breathe and live !

"All joyous in the realms of day."

April Sixteenth.

. . . The path that each man trod
Is dim, or will be dim, with weeds :
What fame is left for human deeds
In endless age ?   It rests with God.

In Memoriam, lxxiii.

April Seventeenth.

God, not man, is the Judge of us all when
life shall cease.

The Grandmother.

April Eighteenth.

Remembering her dear Lord who died for
    all,
And musing on the little lives of men,
And how they mar this little by their feuds.

Sea Dreams.

April Nineteenth.

    Some have striven,
Achieving calm, to whom was given
The joy that mixes man with Heaven.

The Two Voices.

April Twentieth.

Come, Spring! She comes on waste and
    wood,
  On farm and field ; but enter also here,
Diffuse thyself at will thro' all my blood,
  And tho' thy violet sicken into sere,
  Lodge with me all the year!

Progress of Spring.

April Twenty-first.

Can trouble live with April days,
Or sadness in the summer moons?

Bring orchis, bring the foxglove spire,
  The little speedwell's darling blue,
  Deep tulips dash'd with fiery dew,
Laburnums, dropping wells of fire.

In Memoriam, lxxxiii.

April Twenty-second.

Sweet is it to have done the thing one ought,
When fall'n in darker ways.

The Princess.

April Twenty-third.

Ah! when shall all men's good
Be each man's rule, and universal Peace
Lie like a shaft of light across the land,
And like a lane of beams athwart the sea?

The Golden Year.

April Twenty-fourth.

At last I heard a voice upon the slope
Cry to the summit, " Is there any hope? "
To which an answer peal'd from that high
    land,
But in a tongue no man could understand ;
And on the glimmering limit far withdrawn
God made Himself an awful rose of dawn.

The Vision of Sin.

April Twenty-fifth.

New leaf, new life—the days of frost are o'er :
New life, new love to suit the newer day :
New loves are sweet as those that went before.

The Last Tournament.

April Twenty-sixth.

Love's too precious to be lost,
A little grain shall not be spilt.

In Memoriam, lxv.

April Twenty-seventh.

The little rift within the lute,
Or little pitted speck in garner'd fruit,
That rotting inward slowly moulders all.

Vivien.

April Twenty-eighth.

Love that hath us in the net,
Can he pass and we forget?
Many suns arise and set,
Many a chance the years beget.
Love the gift is Love the debt.

The Miller's Daughter.

April Twenty-ninth.

The birds made
Melody on branch and melody in mid-air,
The damp hill-slopes were quicken'd into
green,

And the live green had kindled into flowers,
For it was past the time of Easter-day.

Gareth and Lynette.

April Thirtieth.

Thou hast not true humility,
The highest virtue, mother of them all.

The Holy Grail.

MAY.

May sunshine on May leaves.

VIVIEN.

May First.

A simpler, saner lesson might he learn
  Who reads thy gradual process, Holy
    Spring.
Thy leaves possess the season in their turn,
  And in their time thy warblers rise on
    wing.
How surely glidest thou from March to
  May,
  And changest, breathing it, the sullen
    wind,
Thy scope of operation, day by day,
  Larger and fuller, like the human mind.

Progress of Spring.

May Second.

It is better to fight for the good, than to rail
  at the ill.

Maud.

May Third.

O birds that warble to the morning sky,
O birds that warble as the day goes by,
Sing sweetly.

Gareth and Lynette.

May Fourth.

Now rings the woodland loud and long,
    The distance takes a lovelier hue,
    And drown'd in yonder living blue
The lark becomes a sightless song.

In Memoriam, cxv.

May Fifth.

Our echoes roll from soul to soul,
And grow forever and forever.

The Princess.

May Sixth.

Simple, noble natures, credulous
Of what they long for, good in friend or foe,
There most in those who most have done
   them ill.

Enid.

May Seventh.

Blow trumpet, for the world is white with
   May,
Blow trumpet, the long night hath roll'd
   away!
Blow thro' the living world—" Let the King
   reign!"

The Coming of Arthur.

May Eighth.

They that can wander at will where the
   works of the Lord are reveal'd,
Little guess what joy can be got from a
   cowslip out of the field;

Flowers to these " spirits in prison " are all
they can know of the spring,
They freshen and sweeten the wards like the
waft of an Angel's wing.

In the Children's Hospital.

May Ninth.

Warble, bird, and open flower, and, men
below the dome of azure,
Kneel, adoring Him the Timeless in the flame
that measures Time!

Akbar's Dream.

May Tenth.

The bee buzz'd up in the heat,
" I am faint for your honey, my sweet."
The flower said, " Take it, my dear,
For now is the spring of the year,
So come, come!"
" Hum!"
And the bee buzz'd down from the heat.

The Foresters.

May Eleventh.

The tender grace of a day that is dead
Will never come back to me.

"Break, break, break."

May Twelfth.

Love is hurt with jar and fret,
Love is made a vague regret.

The Miller's Daughter.

May Thirteenth.

Let be thy wail and help thy fellowmen,
And make thy gold thy vassal, not thy king,
And fling free alms into the beggar's bowl,
And send the day into the darken'd heart,
Nor list for guerdon in the voice of men.

The Ancient Sage.

May Fourteenth.

Let the fair white-winged peacemaker fly
To happy havens under all the sky,
And mix the seasons and the golden hours
Till each man finds his own in all men's good,
And all men work in noble brotherhood.

> *Ode sung at the Opening of the*
> *International Exhibition.*

May Fifteenth.

The years with change advance;
If I make dark my countenance,
I shut my life from happier chance.

> *The Two Voices.*

May Sixteenth.

Though world on world in myriad myriads
    roll
Round us, each with different powers,
And other forms of life than ours,
What know we greater than the soul?

> *Ode on the Death of the Duke of Wellington.*

May Seventeenth.

It is the heat and narrowness of the cage
That makes the captive testy ; with free wing
The world were all one Araby.

Queen Mary.

May Eighteenth.

Brother, where two fight
The strongest wins, and truth and love are
strength. ·

Aylmer's Field.

May Nineteenth.

What profit lies in barren faith,
And vacant yearning, though with might
To scale the heaven's highest height,
Or dive below the wells of Death?

In Memoriam, cviii.

May Twentieth.

The fairest flower on earth must fade,
  The brightest hopes on earth must die :
Why should we mourn that man was made
  To droop on earth, but dwell on high?
    " Why should we weep for those who die? "

May Twenty-first.

The wish, that of the living whole
No life may fail beyond the grave,
Derives it not from what we have
The likest God within the soul?
      In Memoriam, lv.

May Twenty-second.

. . . Any man that walks the mead,
  In bud or blade, or bloom, may find,
According as his humors lead,
  A meaning suited to his mind.
        The Day Dream.

May Twenty-third.

Action and reaction,
The miserable see-saw of our child-world,
Make us despise it at odd hours.

Queen Mary.

May Twenty-fourth.

And I must work through months of toil
    And years of cultivation,
Upon my proper patch of soil,
    To grow my own plantation.
I'll take the showers as they fall,
    I will not vex my bosom;
Enough, if at the end of all
    A little garden blossom.

Amphion.

May Twenty-fifth.

Walk on, my soul, nor crouch to agony,
Turn cloud to light, and bitterness to joy,

And dross to gold with glorious alchemy,
Basing the throne above the world's annoy.

Sonnet: "Tho' Night hath climbed."

May Twenty-sixth.

The sun, the moon, the stars
Send no such light upon the ways of men
As one great deed.

Tiresias.

May Twenty-seventh.

I have lived my life, and that which I have
done
May He within Himself make pure!

The Passing of Arthur.

May Twenty-eighth.

Follow you the star that lights a desert path-
way, yours or mine,
Forward, till you see the highest Human
Nature is divine.

Locksley Hall, Sixty Years After.

May Twenty-ninth.

Join hands: let brethren dwell in unity;
Let kith and kin stand close as our shield
    wall;
Who breaks us then?

Harold.

May Thirtieth.

No sound is breathed so potent to coerce,
And to conciliate, as their names who dare
For that sweet motherland which gave them
    birth
Nobly to do, nobly to die. Their names,
Graven on memorial columns, are a song
Heard in the future . . .
. . . their examples reach a hand
Far thro' all years, and everywhere they
    meet
And kindle generous purpose, and the
    strength
To mould it into action pure as theirs.

Tiresias.

May   Thirty-first.

Grateful is the noise of noble deeds
To noble hearts.

Enid.

JUNE.

The wild heather round me, and over me June's
high blue.

JUNE BRACKEN AND HEATHER.

June First.

O dewy flowers that open to the sun,
O dewy flowers that close when day is done,
Blow sweetly.

Gareth and Lynette.

June Second.

A courage to endure and to obey ;
A hate of gossip parlance and of sway.

Isabel.

June Third.

Reign thou above the storms of sorrow and
 ruth
That roar beneath ; unshaken peace hath
 won thee ;
So shalt thou pierce the woven gleams of
 truth,
So shall the blessing of the meek be on
 thee.

Sonnet: " Tho' Night hath climbed."

June Fourth.

I cull from every faith and race the best
And bravest soul for counsellor and friend.

Akbar's Dream.

June Fifth.

Let not Reason fail me, nor the sod
Draw from my death Thy living flower and
grass,
Before I learn that Love, which is and was
My Father, and my Brother, and my God!

Doubt and Prayer.

June Sixth.

Ah, though the times, when some new
thought can bud,
Are but as poets' seasons when they flower,
Yet seas, that daily gain upon the shore,

Have ebb and flow conditioning their march,
And slow and sure comes up the golden
    year.

The Golden Year.

June Seventh.

               From the woods
Came voices of the well-contented doves.
The lark could scarce get out his notes for
    joy,
But shook his song together as he near'd
His happy home, the ground.

The Gardener's Daughter.

June Eighth.

Nature, so far as in her lies,
   Imitates God, and turns her face
To every land beneath the skies,
   Counts nothing that she meets with base,
   But lives and loves in every place.

On a Mourner.

June Ninth.

This life of mine
I guard as God's high gift from scathe and
wrong.

Guinevere.

June Tenth.

The honeysuckle round the porch has wov'n
its wavy bowers,
And by the meadow-trenches blow the faint
sweet cuckoo-flowers.

The May Queen.

June Eleventh.

Sun by sun the happy days
Descend below the golden hills
With promise of a morn as fair.

In Memoriam, lxxxiv.

June Twelfth.

How sweetly smells the honeysuckle !
. . . As if the world were one
Of utter peace, and love, and gentleness!

Gareth and Lynette.

June Thirteenth.

Love is come with a song and a smile,
Welcome Love with a smile and a song :
Love can stay but a little while.
Why cannot he stay? They call him away ;
Ye do him wrong, ye do him wrong ;
Love will stay for a whole life long.

Harold.

June Fourteenth.

Meanwhile, my brothers, work and wield
    The forces of to-day,
And plow the Present like a field,
    And garner all you may.

Mechanophilus.

June Fifteenth.

Were there nothing else
For which to praise the heavens but only
love,
That only love were cause enough for praise.

The Gardener's Daughter.

June Sixteenth.

O happy he, and fit to live,
  On whom a happy home has power
To make him trust his life, and give
  His fealty to the halcyon hour!

The Wanderer.

June Seventeenth.

To pray, to do—
To pray, to do according to the prayer,
Are both to worship Alla, but the prayers
That have no successor in deed are faint
And pale in Alla's eyes.

Akbar's Dream.

June Eighteenth.

Self-reverence, self-knowledge, self-control,
These three alone lead life to sovereign
    power.

Œnone.

June Nineteenth.

A faith as clear as the heights of the June-
    blue heaven,
And a fancy as summer new
As the green of the bracken amid the gloom
    of the heather.

June Bracken and Heather.

June Twentieth.

I can but lift the torch
Of Reason in the dusky cave of Life,
And gaze on this great miracle, the world,
Adoring That who made, and makes, and is.

Akbar's Dream.

June Twenty-first.

Tho' Sin too oft, when smitten by Thy rod,
  Rail at " Blind Fate " with many a vain
  "Alas!"
From sin thro' sorrow into Thee we pass,
By that same path our true forefathers trod.

Doubt and Prayer.

June Twenty-second.

      When creed and race
Shall bear false witness, each of each, no
  more,
But find their limits by that larger light
And overstep them, moving easily
Thro' after-ages in the love of Truth,
And truth of Love.

Akbar's Dream.

June Twenty-third.

Yon, what the cultured surface grows,
  Dispense with careful hands;

Deep unto deep forever goes,
Heaven over heaven expands.

Mechanophilus.

June Twenty-fourth.

Great deeds cannot die;
They with the sun and moon renew their
light
Forever, blessing those that look on them.

The Princess.

June Twenty-fifth.

Nor dream of human love and truth
As dying Nature's earth and lime;
But trust that those we call the dead
Are breathers of an ampler day,
For ever nobler ends.

In Memoriam, cxviii.

June Twenty-sixth.

My own dim life should teach me this,
That life shall live forevermore.

In Memoriam, xxxiv.

June Twenty-seventh.

Nothing can bereave him
Of the force he made his own.

Ode on the Death of the Duke of Wellington.

June Twenty-eighth.

Beauty, Good, and Knowledge are three
sisters
That dote upon each other, friends to man,
Living together under the same roof,
And never can be sunder'd without tears.

To ——: "I send you here."

June Twenty-ninth.

Like men, like manners; like breeds like,
  they say,
Kind nature is the best; those manners next
That fit us like a nature second hand.

Walking to the Mail.

June Thirtieth.

Yet thoroughly to believe in one's own self,
So one's own self be thorough, were to do
Great things.   '

Queen Mary.

JULY.

The gold-lily blows, and overhead
The light cloud smoulders on the summer crag.

EDWIN MORRIS.

July First.

When summer's hourly-mellowing change -
  May breathe, with many roses sweet,
  Upon the thousand waves of wheat
That ripple round the lonely grange.
                 In Memoriam, xci.

July Second.

     He that wrongs his friend
Wrongs himself more, and ever bears about
A silent court of justice in his breast,
Himself the judge and jury, and himself
The prisoner at the bar ever condemned.
                 Sea Dreams.

July Third.

     Live a life of truest breath,
And teach true life to fight with mortal
  wrongs.
                 Maud.

July Fourth.

O Thou that sendest out the man
  To rule by land and sea,
Strong mother of a lion-line,
Be proud of those strong sons of Thine,
  Who wrenched their rights from thee!

What wonder if in noble heat
  Those men thine arms withstood,
Re-taught the lesson thou hadst taught,
And in thy spirit with thee fought—
  Who sprang from noble blood!

England and America in 1782.

July Fifth.

It is the land that freemen till
  That sober-suited Freedom chose,
  The land where girt with friends or foes
A man may speak the thing he will.

" You ask me why, tho' ill at ease."

July Sixth.

What rights are his that dare not strike for
them ?

The Last Tournament.

July Seventh.

We have but faith: we cannot know;
For knowledge is of things we see,
And yet we trust it comes from Thee,
A beam in darkness: let it grow.

In Memoriam.

July Eighth.

O God,
For Thou art merciful, refusing none
That come to Thee for succor, unto Thee,
Therefore I come.

Queen Mary.

July Ninth.

Our wills are ours, we know not how;
Our wills are ours to make them Thine.

In Memoriam.

July Tenth.

Who can say
Why To-day
To-morrow will be yesterday?
Who can tell
Why to smell
The violet recalls the dewy prime
Of youth and buried time?

Song.

July Eleventh.

I would that happiness were gold, that I
Might cast my largess of it to the crowd.

The Cup.

July Twelfth.

Vain, bootless pursuers of honor and fame!
'Tis idle to tell ye, what soon ye must
  prove—
That honor's a bauble, and glory a name,
When put in the balance of friendship and
  love.

> *"Oh ! never may frowns and*
> *dissension molest."*

July Thirteenth.

They said that Love would die when Hope
  was gone,
And Love mourned long and sorrowed after
  Hope ;
At last she sought out Memory, and they
  trod
The same old paths that Love had walked
  with Hope,
And Memory fed the soul of Love with
  tears.

The Lover's Tale.

July Fourteenth.

Meet is it changes should control
  Our being, lest we rust in ease,
  We all are changed by still degrees,
All but the basis of the soul.

"Love thou thy Land."

July Fifteenth.

Ah yet, though all the world forsake,
  Though fortune clip my wings,
I will not cramp my heart, nor take
  Half-views of men and things.

Will Waterproof's Lyrical Monologue.

July Sixteenth.

Whate'er thy joys, they vanish with the day;
Whate'er thy griefs, in sleep they fade away.

The Foresters.

July Seventeenth.

If we change at all
We needs must do it quickly ; it is an age
Of brief life, and brief purpose, and brief
patience.

Queen Mary.

July Eighteenth.

This thing, that thing is the rage,
Helter-skelter runs the age ;
Minds on this round earth of ours
Vary like the leaves and flowers
Fashion'd after certain laws.

Poets and Critics.

July Nineteenth.

And what delights can equal those
That stir the spirit's inner deeps,
When one that loves, but knows not, reaps
A truth from one that loves and knows.

In Memoriam, xlii.

July Twentieth.

The silent blessing of one honest man
Is heard in Heaven.

The Foresters.

July Twenty-first.

When men are tost
On tides of strange opinion, and not sure
Of their own selves, they are wroth with
their own selves
And thence with others.

Queen Mary.

July Twenty-second.

He that shuts Love out, in turn shall be
Shut out from Love, and on her threshold lie
Howling in outer darkness.   Not for this
Was common clay ta'en from the common
earth,

Moulded by God, and temper'd with the
tears
Of angels to the perfect shape of man.

To —— "I send you here."

July Twenty-third.

Love took up the harp of Life, and smote
on all the chords with might ;
Smote the chord of Self, that, trembling,
pass'd in music out of sight.

Locksley Hall.

July Twenty-fourth.

Thrice blest whose lives are faithful prayers,
Whose loves in higher love endure ;
What souls possess themselves so pure,
Or is there blessedness like theirs?

In Memoriam, xxxii.

July Twenty-fifth.

Love is and was my King and Lord,
  And will be, tho' as yet I keep
  Within his court on earth, and sleep
Encompass'd by his faithful guard,

And hear at times a sentinel
  Who moves about from place to place,
  And whispers to the worlds of space,
In the deep night, that all is well.

In Memoriam, cxxvi.

July Twenty-sixth.

Thou dost ever brood above
The silence of all hearts, unutterable Love.

Love.

July Twenty-seventh.

Oh! sure it is a special care
Of God, to fortify from doubt,

To arm in proof and guard about
With triple mailèd trust.

Supposed Confessions.

July Twenty-eighth.

Steel me with patience! soften me with
grief!
Let blow the trumpet strongly while I pray,
Till this embattled wall of unbelief,
My prison, not my fortress, fall away.
Then if Thou willest let my day be brief,
So Thou wilt strike Thy glory through the
day.

Doubt and Prayer.

July Twenty-ninth.

Live pure, speak true, right wrong, follow
the King—
Else, wherefore born?

Gareth and Lynette.

July Thirtieth.

Is He not yonder in those uttermost
Parts of the morning? if I flee to these
Can I go from Him? and the sea is His,
The sea is His: He made it.

Enoch Arden.

July Thirty-first.

The wages of sin is death: if the wages of
  Virtue be dust,
  Would she have heart to endure for the
  life of the worm and the fly?
She desires no isles of the blest, no quiet
  seats of the just,
  To rest in a golden grove, or to bask in
  a summer sky:
Give her the wages of going on, and not to
  die.

Wages.

AUGUST.

All in the blue unclouded weather.

THE LADY OF SHALOTT.

August First.

He fought his doubts and gather'd strength,
He would not make his judgment blind,
He faced the spectres of the mind
And laid them.

In Memoriam, xcvi.

August Second.

Go forth, . . .
And break thro' all, till One will crown thee
king
Far in the spiritual city.

The Holy Grail.

August Third.

And when thou sendest thy free soul thro'
heaven,
Nor understandest bound nor boundlessness,
Thou seest the Nameless of the hundred
Names!

The Ancient Sage.

August Fourth.

Doubt no longer that the Highest is the
    wisest and the best,
Let not all that saddens Nature blight thy
    hope or break thy rest.
Quail not at the fiery mountain, at the ship-
    wreck, or the rolling
Thunder, or the rending earthquake, or the
    famine or the pest!

Faith.

August Fifth.

No compound of this earthly ball
Is like another, all in all.

The Two Voices.

August Sixth.

Flower, in the crannied wall,
I pluck you out of the crannies,—
Hold you here, root and all, in my hand,

Little flower,—but if I could understand
What you are, root and all, and all in all,
I should know what God and man is.

"Flower in the crannied wall."

August Seventh.

Strong Son of God, immortal Love,
  Whom we, that have not seen Thy face,
  By faith, and faith alone embrace,
Believing where we cannot prove.

In Memoriam.

August Eighth.

O diviner Light,
  Thro' the cloud that roofs our noon with
    night,
Thro' the blotting mist, the blinding showers,
  Far from out a sky forever bright,
Over all the woodland's flooded bowers,
Over all the meadow's drowning flowers,
Over all this ruin'd world of ours,
  Break, diviner Light!

The Sisters.

August Ninth.

Heaven and earth are threads of the same
loom.

Harold.

August Tenth.

See thou, that countest reason ripe,
  In holding by the law within,
  Thou fail not in a world of sin.

In Memoriam, xxxiii.

August Eleventh.

Not sowing hedgerow texts and passing by,
Nor dealing goodly counsel from a height
That makes the lowest hate it, but a voice
Of comfort and an open hand of help.

Aylmer's Field.

August Twelfth.

When one small touch of Charity
Could lift them nearer Godlike state,
Than if the crowded Orb should cry
Like those that cried Diana great.

Literary Squabbles.

August Thirteenth.

What keeps a spirit wholly true
To that ideal which he bears?
What record?

In Memoriam, lii.

August Fourteenth.

Few there be
So gross of heart who have not felt and
known
A higher than they see.

Timbuctoo.

August Fifteenth.

The Peak is high and flush'd
At his highest with sunrise fire:
The Peak is high, and the stars are high,
And the thought of a man is higher.

The Voice and the Peak.

August Sixteenth.

He came at length
To find a stronger faith his own;
And Power was with him in the night,
Which makes the darkness and the light,
And dwells not in the light alone,
But in the darkness and the cloud,
As over Sinai's peaks of old.

In Memoriam, xcvi.

August Seventeenth.

The goal of this great world
Lies beyond sight.

To the Queen.

August Eighteenth.

The world were wholly fair,
But that these eyes of men are dense and
dim,
And have not power to see it as it is,
Perchance because we see not to the close.

The Passing of Arthur.

August Nineteenth.

Neither mourn if human creeds be lower
than the heart's desire!
Through the gates that bar the distance
comes a gleam of what is higher.
Wait till Death has flung them open, when
the man will make the Maker
Dark no more with human hatreds in the
glare of deathless fire!

Faith.

August Twentieth.

Faith and unfaith can ne'er be equal powers :
Unfaith in aught is want of faith in all.

Vivien.

August Twenty-first.

More things are wrought by prayer
Than this world dreams of.   Wherefore, let
    thy voice
Rise like a fountain for me night and day.

The Passing of Arthur.

August Twenty-second.

The soul of the woods hath stricken thro'
    my blood,
The love of freedom, the desire of God,
The hope of larger life hereafter.

The Foresters.

August Twenty-third.

That every morning . . .
May be most good, is every morning's
prayer.

Queen Mary.

August Twenty-fourth.

Cast the poison from your bosom, oust the
madness from your brain.
Let the trampled serpent show you that you
have not lived in vain.

Locksley Hall, Sixty Years after.

August Twenty-fifth.

The fire of Heaven is on the dusty ways,
The wayside blossoms open to the blaze ;
The whole wood-world is one full peal of
praise.

Balin and Balan.

August Twenty-sixth.

Nor thou be rageful, like a handled bee,
And lose thy life by usage of thy sting;
Nor harm an adder thro' the lust for harm,
And more—think well! Do well will follow
    thought.

The Ancient Sage.

August Twenty-seventh.

. . . While we breathe beneath the sun,
  The world which credits what is done
Is cold to all that might have been.

In Memoriam, lxxv.

August Twenty-eighth.

On either side the river lie
Long fields of barley and of rye,
That clothe the wold and meet the sky.

The Lady of Shalott.

August Twenty-ninth.

A second voice was at mine ear,
A little whisper silver-clear,
A murmur, " Be of better cheer."

The Two Voices.

August Thirtieth.

No lapse of moons can canker Love,
Whatever fickle tongues may say.

In Memoriam, xxvi.

August Thirty-first.

Over! the sweet summer closes,
   And never a flower at the close ;
Over and gone with the roses,
   And winter again and the snows.

Becket.

SEPTEMBER.

Autumn laying here and there
A fiery finger on the leaves.

IN MEMORIAM, XCIX.

September First.

And blessings on the falling out
    That all the more endears,
When we fall out with those we love
    And kiss again with tears!

The Princess.

September Second.

Most blameless is he, centred in the sphere
Of common duties.

Ulysses.

September Third.

So fret not, like an idle girl,
    That life is dash'd with flecks of sin.
    Abide: thy wealth is gather'd in,
When Time hath sunder'd shell from pearl.

In Memoriam, lii.

September Fourth.

When will the stream be aweary of flowing
　　Under my eye?
When will the wind be aweary of blowing
　　Over the sky?
When will the clouds be aweary of fleeting?
When will the heart be aweary of beating,
　　And nature die?
Never, oh! never, nothing will die.

Nothing Will Die.

September Fifth.

So many worlds, so much to do,
　So little done, such things to be!

In Memoriam, lxxiii.

September Sixth.

Love of God and men
And noble deeds, the flower of all the world.

Vivien.

September Seventh.

. . . To me is given
Such hope, I know not fear;
I yearn to breathe the airs of heaven
That often meet me here.

Sir Galahad.

September Eighth.

Above the perilous seas of Change and
Chance
. . . hold out the lights of cheerfulness,
As the tall ship, that many a dreary year
Knit to some dismal sand-bank far at sea,
All thro' the livelong hours of utter dark,
Showers slanting light upon the dolorous
wave.

The Lover's Tale.

September Ninth.

There lie two ways to every end,
A better and a worse.

Queen Mary.

September Tenth.

In that hour
From out my sullen heart a power
Broke, like the rainbow from the shower,

To feel, altho' no tongue can prove,
That every cloud that spreads above
And veileth love, itself is love.

The Two Voices.

September Eleventh.

Follow Light and do the Right—for man
can half control his doom—
Till you find the deathless Angel seated in
the vacant tomb.

Locksley Hall, Sixty Years After.

September Twelfth.

It is the little rift within the lute,
That by and by will make the music mute,
And ever widening slowly silence all.

Vivien.

September Thirteenth.

The varying leaf with blade and sheaf
Clothes and reclothes the happy plains.

The Day Dream.

September Fourteenth.

To do him any wrong was to beget
A kindness from him, for his heart was rich,
Of such fine mould, that if you sow'd
  therein
The seed of Hate, it blossom'd Charity.

Queen Mary.

September Fifteenth.

Autumn, with a noise of rooks
That gather in the waning woods.

In Memoriam, lxxxv.

September Sixteenth.

That loss is common would not make
  My own less bitter, rather more:
  Too common!   Never morning wore
To evening but some heart did break.

In Memoriam, vi.

September Seventeenth.

If utter darkness closed the day,—
But earth's dark forehead flings athwart the
    heaven
Her shadow crown'd with stars—and yonder
    —out
To northward—some that never set but pass
From sight and night to lose themselves in
    day.

The Ancient Sage.

September Eighteenth.

The love that rose on stronger wings,
   Unpalsied when we met with Death,
   Is comrade of the lesser faith
That sees the course of human things.

In Memoriam, cxxviii.

September Nineteenth.

For who can always act? but he,
   To whom a thousand memories call,
   Not being less but more than all,
The gentleness he seem'd to be.

In Memoriam, cxi.

September Twentieth.

And, because right is right, to follow right
Were wisdom in the scorn of consequence.

Œnone.

September Twenty-first.

By the rude blasts of passion tost,
We sigh for bliss we ne'er had lost,
　Had Conscience been our guide;
She burns a lamp we need not trim,
Whose steady flame is never dim,
　But throws its lustre wide.

"Religion tho' we seem to spurn."

September Twenty-second.

And the bee buzz'd up in the cold,
When the flower was wither'd and old;
" Have you still any honey, my dear? "
She said, " It's the fall of the year,
　But come, come! "
　　" Hum! "
And the bee buzz'd off in the cold.

The Foresters.

September Twenty-third.

Many so dote upon this bubble world,
Whose colors in a moment break and fly,
They care for nothing else.

Queen Mary.

September Twenty-fourth.

He hath no thought of coming woes,
He hath no care of life or death,
Scarce outward signs of joy arise,
Because the Spirit of happiness
And perfect rest so inward is.

Supposed Confessions.

September Twenty-fifth.

What time I wasted youthful hours,
One of the shining wingèd powers
Show'd me vast cliffs with crown of towers.

.   .   .   .   .

He said, "The labor is not small;
Yet winds the pathway free to all :—
Take care thou dost not fear to fall!"

Stanzas—"What time I wasted."

September Twenty-sixth.

Victor from vanquish'd issues at the last,
And overthrower from being overthrown.

Gareth and Lynette.

September Twenty-seventh.

A man may fail in duty twice,
And the third time may prosper.

The Passing of Arthur.

September Twenty-eighth.

For tho' from out our bourne of Time and
Place
The flood may bear me far,

I hope to see my Pilot face to face,
When I have crost the bar.

Crossing the Bar.

September Twenty-ninth.

Hold thou the good: define it well.

In Memoriam, liii.

September Thirtieth.

Our little systems have their day;
They have their day and cease to be:
They are but broken lights of Thee,
And Thou, O Lord, art more than they!

In Memoriam.

OCTOBER.

Through the faded leaf
The chestnut pattering to the ground.

In Memoriam, xi.

October First.

Calm and still light on yon great plain
That sweeps with all its autumn bowers,
And crowded farms and lessening towers,
To mingle with the bounding main.

In Memoriam, xi.

October Second.

Gain in life, as life advances;
Valor and charity more and more.

To the Rev. F. D. Maurice.

October Third.

God bless thee . . .
With blessings beyond hope or thought,
With blessings which no word can find.

The Miller's Daughter.

October Fourth.

Manners are not idle, but the fruit
Of loyal nature, and of noble mind.

Guinevere.

October Fifth.

Man for the field and woman for the hearth;
Man for the sword and for the needle she;
Man with the head and woman with the
heart;
Man to command and woman to obey;
All else confusion.

The Princess.

October Sixth.

O well for him whose will is strong!
He suffers, but he will not suffer long;
He suffers, but he cannot suffer wrong.

Will.

October Seventh.

Life is not as idle ore,
But iron dug from central gloom,
And heated hot with burning fears,
And dipt in baths of hissing tears,
And batter'd with the shocks of doom
To shape and use.

In Memoriam, cxviii.

October Eighth.

Most of sterling worth is what
Our own experience preaches.

Will Waterproof's Lyrical Monologue.

October Ninth.

She walk'd
Wearing the light yoke of that Lord of love
Who still'd the rolling wave of Galilee.

Aylmer's Field.

October Tenth.

It is man's privilege to doubt,
If so be that from doubt, at length,
Truth may stand forth unmoved of change.

Supposed Confessions.

October Eleventh.

There lives more faith in honest doubt,
Believe me, than in half the creeds.

In Memoriam, xcvi.

October Twelfth.

. . . Like a child in doubt and fear:
But that blind clamor made me wise;
Then was I as a child that cries,
But, crying, knows his father near.

In Memoriam, cxxiv.

October Thirteenth.

If thou would'st hear the Nameless, and wilt
    dive
Into the temple cave of thine own self,
There, brooding by the central altar, thou
May'st haply learn the Nameless hath a voice,
By which thou wilt abide if thou be wise.

The Ancient Sage.

October Fourteenth.

There is no mightier Spirit than I to sway
The heart of man ; and teach him to attain
By shadowing forth the Unattainable ;
And step by step to scale that mighty stair
Whose landing-place is wrapt about with
    clouds
Of glory of heaven.

Timbuctoo.

October Fifteenth.

The fire of Heaven is lord of all things good,
And starve not thou this fire within thy blood.

Balin and Balan.

October Sixteenth.

The days and hours are ever glancing by,
And seem to flicker past thro' sun and shade,
Or short, or long, as Pleasure leads or Pain.

The Ancient Sage.

October Seventeenth.

Live thy Life,
  Young and old,
Like yon oak,
Bright in spring
  Living gold.

Summer rich
  Then; and then

Autumn-changed,

Soberer-hued,

Gold again.

The Oak.

October Eighteenth.

Here too much

We moulder—as to things without, I mean.

The Holy Grail.

October Nineteenth.

Hearted with hope, of hope as full

As is the blood with life, or night

And a dark cloud with rich moonlight.

Supposed Confessions.

October Twentieth.

This is truth the poet sings,

That a sorrow's crown of sorrow is remem-

bering happier things.

Locksley Hall.

October Twenty-first.

But truth, they say, will out,
So it must last.   It is not like a word
That comes and goes in uttering.

Queen Mary.

October Twenty-second.

I let men worship as they will, I reap
No revenue from the field of unbelief.

Akbar's Dream.

October Twenty-third.

He was not all unhappy.   His resolve
Upbore him, and firm faith, and evermore
Prayer from a living source within the will,
And beating up thro' all the bitter world,
Like fountains of sweet water in the sea,
Kept him a living soul.

Enoch Arden.

October Twenty-fourth.

There's somewhat in this world amiss
Shall be unriddled by and by.

The Miller's Daughter.

October Twenty-fifth.

Dark is the world to thee; thyself is the reason why,
For is He not all but thou, that hast power
to feel " I am I "?
Speak to Him, thou, for He hears, and Spirit
with Spirit can meet—
Closer is He than breathing and nearer than
hands and feet.

The Higher Pantheism.

October Twenty-sixth.

Wearing the white flower of a blameless life,
Before a thousand peering littlenesses.

Dedication of the Idylls of the King.

October Twenty-seventh.

The wind that beats the mountain, blows
More softly round the open wold ;
And gently comes the world to those
Who are cast in a gentle mould.

To J. S.

October Twenty-eighth.

Wait, and Love himself will bring
The drooping flower of knowledge changed
to fruit
Of Wisdom. Wait : my faith is large in Time
And that which shapes it to some perfect
end.

Love and Duty.

October Twenty-ninth.

Let there be thistles, there are grapes ;
If old things, there are new ;

Ten thousand broken lights and shapes,
  Yet glimpses of the true.
    Will Waterproof's Lyrical Monologue.

October Thirtieth.

We feel we are nothing—for all is Thou and
  in Thee;
We feel we are something—that also has
  come from Thee.
We are nothing, O Thou—but Thou wilt
  help us to be!
    De Profundis.

October Thirty-first.

What time the mighty moon was gathering
  light,
Love paced the thymy plots of Paradise,
And all about him roll'd his lustrous eyes;

When, turning round a cassia, full in view
Death, walking all alone beneath a yew,
And talking to himself, first met his sight;
"You must begone," said Death, "these
    walks are mine."
Love wept and spread his sheeny vans for
    flight;
Yet ere he parted said, "This hour is thine:
Thou art the shadow of life, and as the tree
Stands in the sun and shadows all beneath,
So in the light of great eternity
Life eminent creates the shade of death;
The shadow passeth when the tree shall fall,
But I shall reign forever over all."

Love and Death.

NOVEMBER.

> The chill
> November dawns and dewy-glooming downs,
> The gentle shower, the smell of dying leaves,
> And the low moan of leaden-color'd seas.
>
> ENOCH ARDEN.

November First.

Down with ambition, avarice, pride,
Jealousy, down! cut off from the mind
The bitter springs of anger and fear;
Down, too, down at your own fireside,
With the evil tongue and the evil ear,
For each is at war with mankind.

Maud.

November Second.

On God and Godlike men we build our trust.
Ode on the Death of the Duke of Wellington.

November Third.

There surely lives in man and beast
Something divine to warn them of their foes.

Sea Dreams.

November Fourth.

The woods are hush'd, their music is no more,
The leaf is dead.

The Last Tournament.

November Fifth.

Rich in saving common-sense,
And, as the greatest only are,
In his simplicity sublime.

Ode on the Death of the Duke of Wellington.

November Sixth.

. . . Each by turns was guide to each,
And Fancy light from Fancy caught,
And Thought leapt out to wed with
Thought,
Ere Thought could wed itself with Speech.

In Memoriam, xxiii.

November Seventh.

Let me fly discaged to sweep
In ever-highering eagle-circles up
To the great Sun of Glory, and thence swoop
Down upon all things base, and dash them
    dead.

Gareth and Lynette.

November Eighth.

The soldier, when he lets his whole self go,
Lost in the common good, the common
    wrong,
Strikes truest ev'n for his own self.

Becket.

November Ninth.

As we surpass our fathers' skill
    Our sons will shame our own;
A thousand things are hidden still
    And not a hundred known.

And had some prophet spoken true
Of all we shall achieve,
The wonders were so wildly new
That no man would believe.

Mechanophilus.

November Tenth.

Who love best have best the grace to know
That Love by right divine is deathless king.

Duke and Duchess of Edinburgh.

November Eleventh.

. . . I am sure that some of our children
would die
But for the voice of Love, and the smile,
and the comforting eye.

In the Children's Hospital.

November Twelfth.

. . . They tell me that the world is hard, and
    harsh of mind;

But can it be so hard, so harsh, as those that
    should be kind?

That matters not: let come what will; at
    last the end is sure,

And every heart that loves with truth is
    equal to endure.

The Flight.

November Thirteenth.

The winds begin to rise
And roar from yonder dropping day;
The last red leaf is whirl'd away,
The rooks are blown about the skies.

In Memoriam, xv.

November Fourteenth.

The loss that brought us pain,
That loss but made us love the more.

The Miller's Daughter.

November Fifteenth.

For all the souls on earth that live
To be forgiven must forgive.
Forgive him seventy times and seven:
For all the blessed souls in Heaven
Are both forgivers and forgiven.

The Promise of May.

November Sixteenth.

On the nigh-naked tree the robin piped
Disconsolate, and thro' the dripping haze
The dead weight of the dead leaf bore it
      down:
Thicker the drizzle grew, deeper the gloom.

Enoch Arden.

November Seventeenth.

Alchemize old hates into the gold
Of Love and make it current.

Akbar's Dream.

November Eighteenth.

We sleep and wake and sleep, but all things
    move ;
The Sun flies forward to his brother Sun ;
The dark Earth follows wheel'd in her ellipse ;
And human things returning on themselves
Move onward, leading up the golden year.

The Golden Year.

November Nineteenth.

The beauty that endures on the Spiritual
    height,
    When we shall stand transfigured, like
        Christ on Hermon hill,
And moving each to music, soul in soul and
    light in light,
    Shall flash through one another in a mo-
        ment as we will.

Happy.

November Twentieth.

The miserable have no medicine
But only Hope.

Romney's Remorse.

November Twenty-first.

Whatever crazy sorrow saith,
No life that breathes with human breath
Has ever truly longed for death.

The Two Voices.

November Twenty-second.

The wealth of waters might but seem to draw
From yon dark cave, but, son, the source is
    higher,
Yon summit half-a-league in air—and higher,
The cloud that hides it—higher still, the
    heavens

Whereby the cloud was moulded, and where-
out

The cloud descended.   Force is from the
height.

The Ancient Sage.

November Twenty-third.

Methinks most men are but poor-hearted,
else

Should we so dote on courage, were it com-
moner?

Queen Mary.

November Twenty-fourth.

Far away beyond her myriad coming changes
Earth will be

Something other than the wildest modern
guess of you and me.

Locksley Hall, Sixty Years After.

November Twenty-fifth.

Till you should turn to dearer matters,
Dear to the man that is dear to God;
How best to help the slender store,
How mend the dwellings of the poor.

To the Rev. F. D. Maurice.

November Twenty-sixth.

I pray you all to love together
Like brethren; yet what hatred Christian
   men
Bear to each other, seeming not as brethren
But mortal foes!   But do you good to all
As much as in you lieth.

Queen Mary.

November Twenty-seventh.

The winds were in the beech:
We heard them sweep the winter land.

In Memoriam, xxx.

November Twenty-eighth.

All precious things, discover'd late,
To those that seek them issue forth;
For love in sequel works with fate,
And draws the veil from hidden worth.

The Day Dream.

November Twenty-ninth.

We move, the wheel must always move,
    Not always on the plain,
And if we move to such a goal
    As Wisdom hopes to gain:
Then you that drive and know your Craft
    Will firmly hold the rein,
Nor lend an ear to random cries
    Or you may drive in vain.

Politics.

November Thirtieth.

Our short-lived sun, before his winter plunge,
Laughs at the last red leaf, and Andrew's
day.

Queen Mary.

DECEMBER.

'Tis the world's winter.

NOTHING WILL DIE.

December First.

Nay, the world, the world,
All ear and eye, with such a stupid heart
To interpret ear and eye, and such a tongue
To blare its own interpretation.

Elaine.

December Second.

Wisdom, when in power
And wisest, should not frown as power, but
smile .
As kindness, watching all till the true *must*
Shall make her strike as Power.

Harold.

December Third.

Teach high thought, and amiable words
And courtliness, and the desire of fame,
And love of truth, and all that makes a man.

Guinevere.

December Fourth.

This fine old world of ours is but a child
Yet in the go-cart. Patience! Give it time
To learn its limbs: there is a hand that
    guides.

The Princess.

December Fifth.

I will not shut me from my kind,
    And, lest I stiffen into stone,
    I will not eat my heart alone,
Nor feed with sighs a passing wind.

In Memoriam, cviii.

December Sixth.

The streets are dumb with snow.

Sir Galahad.

December Seventh.

How many among us at this very hour
Do forge a lifelong trouble for ourselves
By taking true for false or false for true.

Enid.

December Eighth.

Knowledge is now no more a fountain seal'd :
Drink deep, until the habits of the slave,
The sins of emptiness, gossip, and spite,
And slander die.

The Princess.

December Ninth.

Turn, Fortune, turn thy wheel with smile or
frown ;
With that wild wheel we go not up or down ;
Our hoard is little, but our hearts are great.

Enid.

December Tenth.

On this whirligig of Time
We circle with the seasons.

Will Waterproof's Lyrical Monologue.

December Eleventh.

For what are men better than sheep or goats
That nourish a blind life within the brain,
If, knowing God, they lift not hands of prayer
Both for themselves and those who call them
    friend?
For so the whole round earth is every way
Bound by gold chains about the feet of God.

The Passing of Arthur.

December Twelfth.

Glory of Virtue, to fight, to struggle, to right
    the wrong—
Nay, but she aim'd not at glory, no lover of
    glory she :
Give her the glory of going on, and still to be.

Wages.

December Thirteenth.

How dull it is to pause, to make an end,
To rust unburnish'd, not to shine in use!
As though to breathe were Life.

Ulysses.

December Fourteenth.

O living Will that shalt endure
When all that seems shall suffer shock,
Rise in the spiritual rock,
Flow thro' our deeds and make them pure.

In Memoriam, cxxxi.

December Fifteenth.

The simple, silent, honest man
Is worth a world of tonguesters.

Harold.

December Sixteenth.

Love thou thy land, with love far-brought
From out the storied Past, and used
Within the Present, but transfused
Thro' future time by power of thought.

"Love thou thy land."

December Seventeenth.

There's not a flower on all the hills; the
frost is on the pane.

The Queen of the May.

December Eighteenth.

He that walks . . . only thirsting
For the right, and learns to deaden
Love of self, before his journey closes,
He shall find the stubborn thistle bursting
Into glossy purples which outredden
All voluptuous garden-roses.

Ode on the Death of the Duke of Wellington.

December Nineteenth.

O well for him that finds a friend,
Or makes a friend where'er he come,
And loves the world from end to end!

The Wanderer.

December Twentieth.

The sin

That neither God nor man can well forgive,
Hypocrisy.

Sea Dreams.

December Twenty-first.

And all is well, though faith and form
  Be sunder'd in the night of fear;
  Well roars the storm to those that hear
A deeper voice across the storm.

In Memoriam, cxxvii.

December Twenty-second.

Time driveth onward fast,
And in a little while our lips are dumb.

The Lotos-Eaters.

December Twenty-third.

O summer leaf, isn't life as brief?
But this is the time of hollies,
And my heart, my heart is an evergreen;
I hate the spites and the follies.

On a Spiteful Letter.

December Twenty-fourth.

The time draws near the birth of Christ:
The moon is hid; the night is still;
The Christmas bells from hill to hill
Answer each other in the mist.

In Memoriam, xxviii.

December Twenty-fifth.

Rise, happy morn, rise, holy morn,
　　Draw forth the cheerful day from night;
　　O Father, touch the east, and light
The light that shone when Hope was born.

In Memoriam, xxx.

December Twenty-sixth.

Men, my brothers, men the workers, ever
　　reaping something new;
That which they have done but earnest of
　　the things that they shall do.

Locksley Hall.

December Twenty-seventh.

A spirit haunts the year's last hours
Dwelling amid these yellowing bowers:
　　To himself he talks;
For at eventide, listening earnestly,

At his work you may hear him sob and sigh
  In the walks;
  Earthward he boweth the heavy stalks
Of the mouldering flowers.

Song.

December Twenty-eighth.

Ill for him who, bettering not with time,
Corrupts the strength of heaven-descended
  Will.

Will.

December Twenty-ninth.

The sin that practice burns into the blood,
And not the one dark hour which brings re-
  morse,
Will brand us, after, of whose fold we be.

Vivien.

December Thirtieth.

Full knee-deep lies the winter snow,
And the winter winds are wearily sighing:

Toll ye the church-bell sad and slow,
And tread softly and speak low,
For the old year lies a-dying!

The Death of the Old Year.

December Thirty-first.

Ring out, wild bells, to the wild sky,
The flying cloud, the frosty light:
The year is dying in the night;
Ring out, wild bells, and let him die.

Ring out the old, ring in the new,
Ring, happy bells, across the snow:
The year is going, let him go;
Ring out the false, ring in the true.

In Memoriam, cvi